My Mummy is an Aviator
Copyright © 2023 by Talula Grey

All rights reserved.
No part of this publication may be reproduced, distributed, or transmitted in any form or by any means, including photocopying, recording, or other electronic or mechanical methods, without the prior written permission of the publisher, except as permitted by U.S.A & U.K. copyright law. For permission requests, contact Bianca Robbins Publishing via TalulaGrey.com.
The story, all names, characters, and incidents portrayed in this production are fictitious. No identification with actual persons (living or deceased), places, buildings, and products is intended or should be inferred.

My Mummy's an AVIATOR

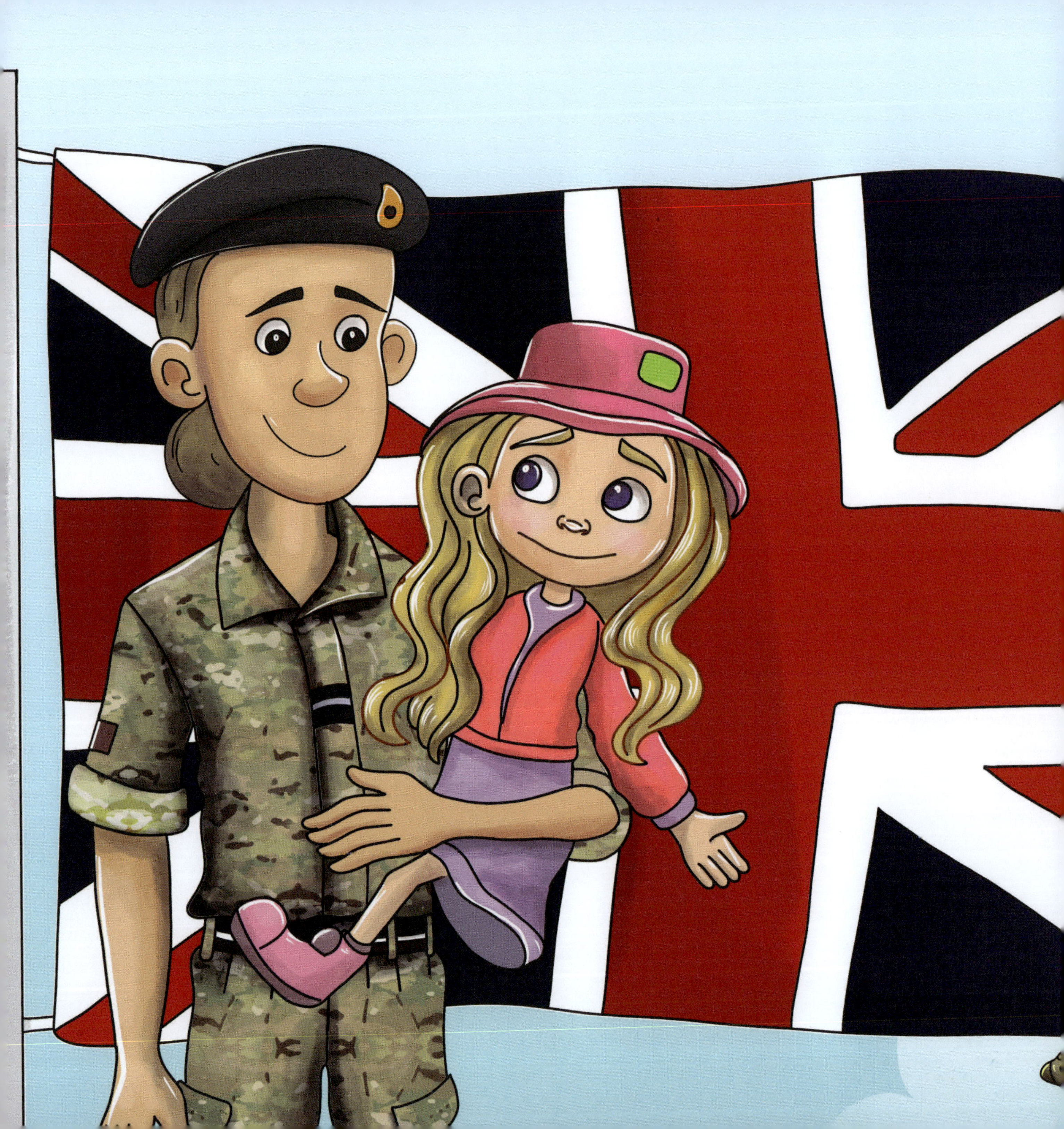

My mummy's away on an operation,
for 6 months in a foreign location.
She's an aviator in the Royal Air Force,
using Air Power to protect us all.
Mummy's been sent on an important mission,
to show off our might, representing the United Kingdom.

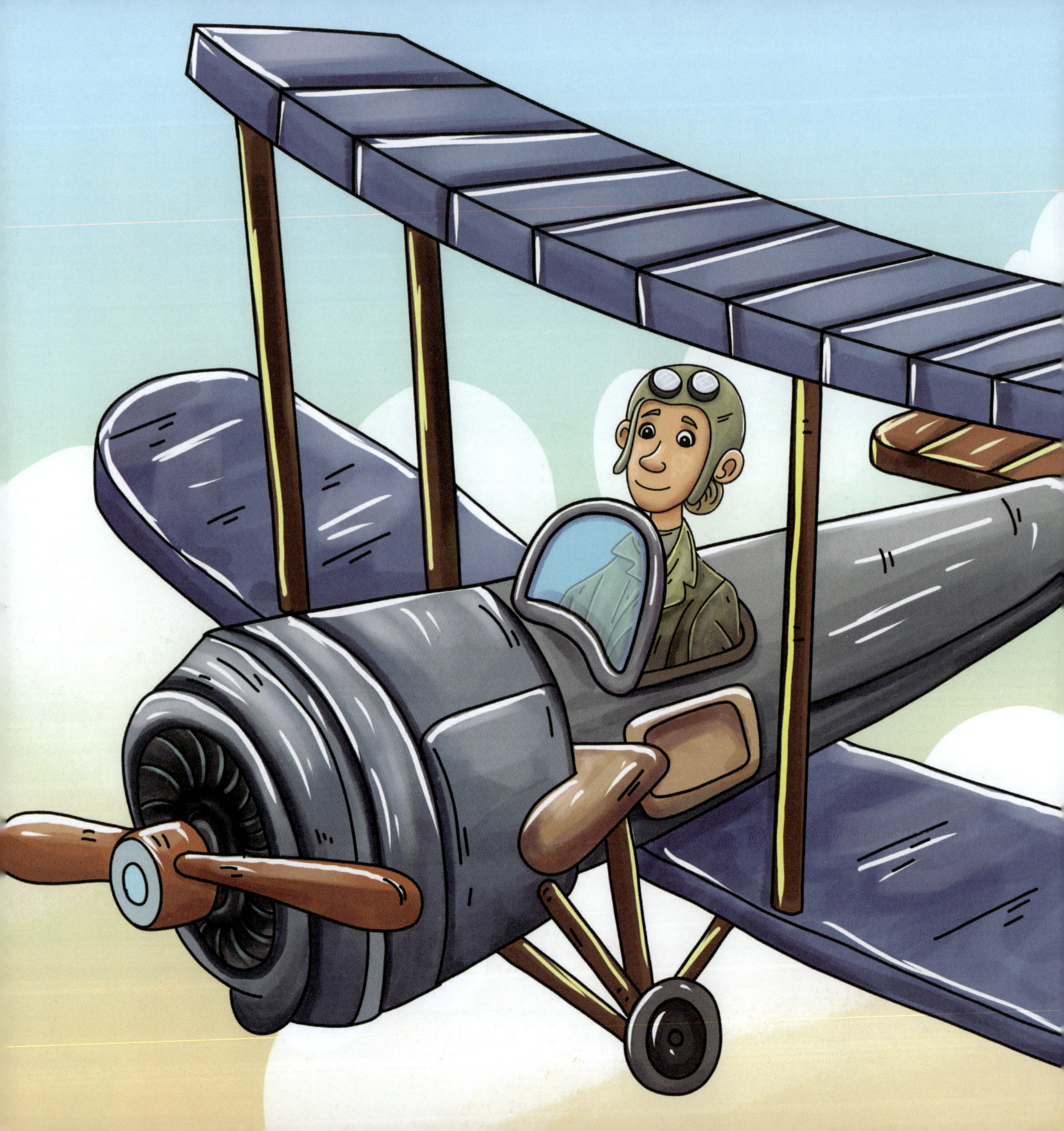

The RAF, established in 1918,
the first independent Air Force the world had seen.
They have pilots to fly their aircraft high,
like helicopters and jets soaring in the sky.
Engineers, medical staff, chefs and whole
teams of computer experts and air traffic control.

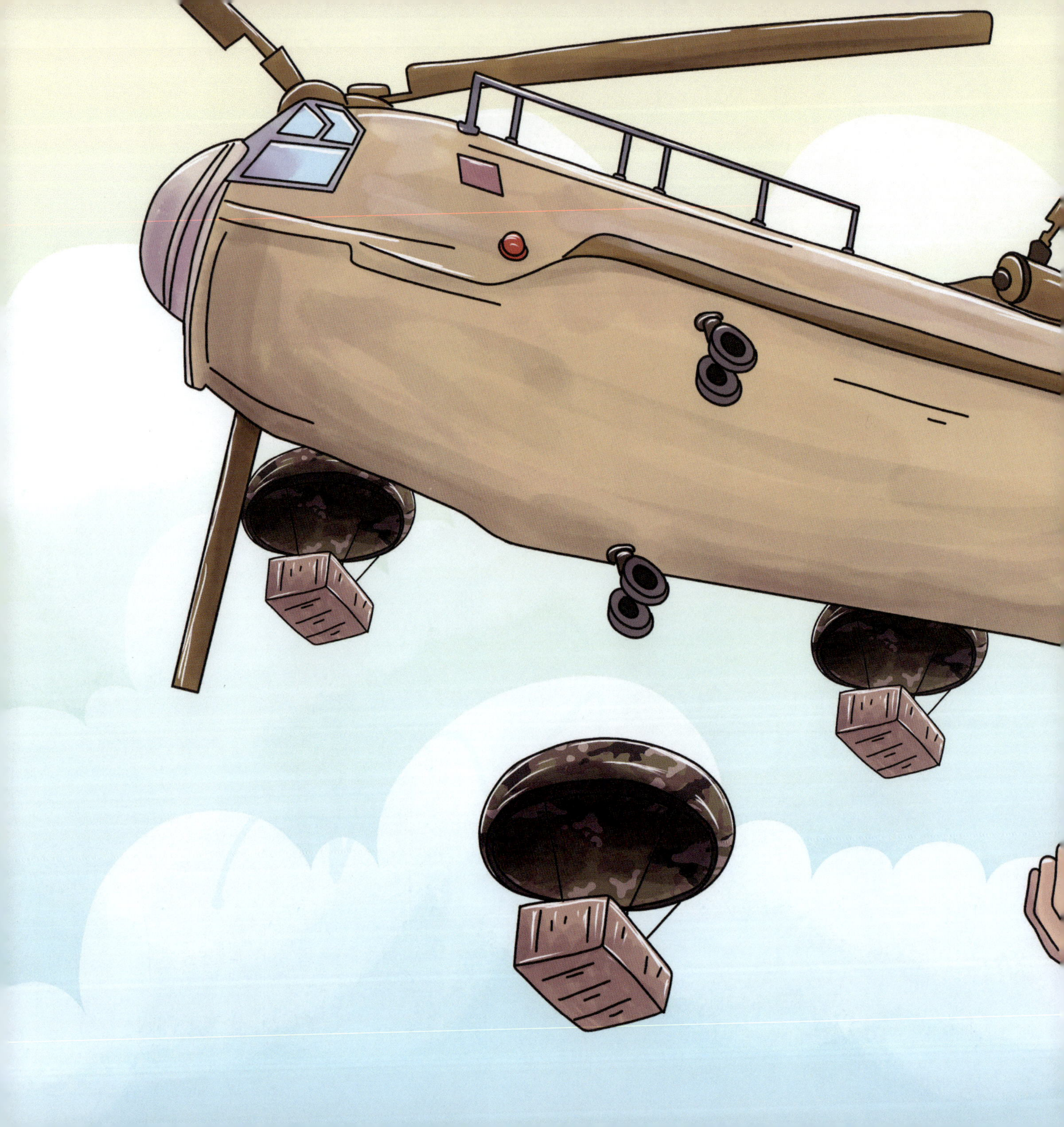

My mummy's a hero, saving people in need,
delivering food and medical supplies with speed.
From disasters like hurricanes and tidal waves,
helicopters evacuate people who need to be saved.
The Royal Air Force never fails,
when it comes to delivering humanitarian aid.

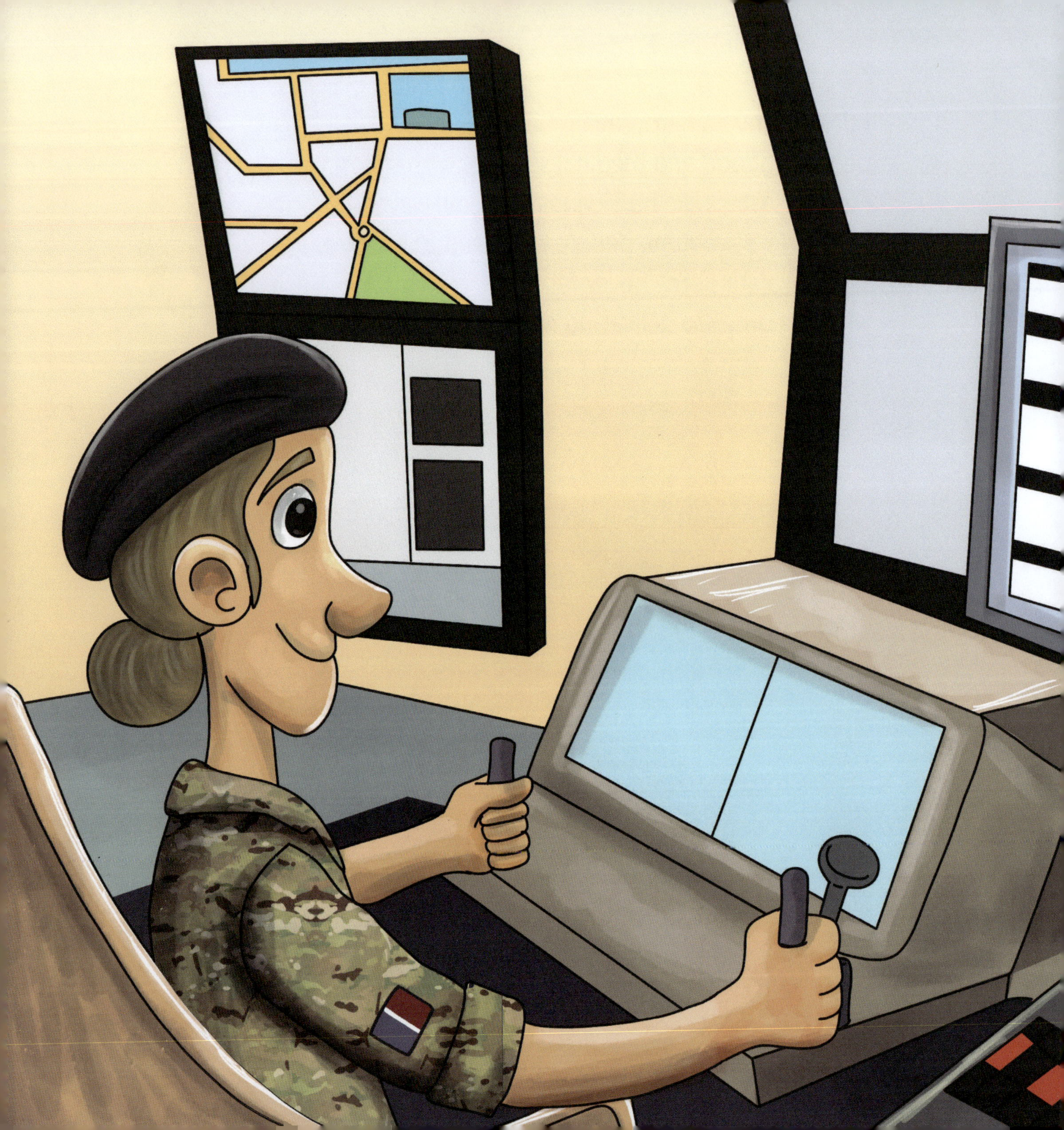

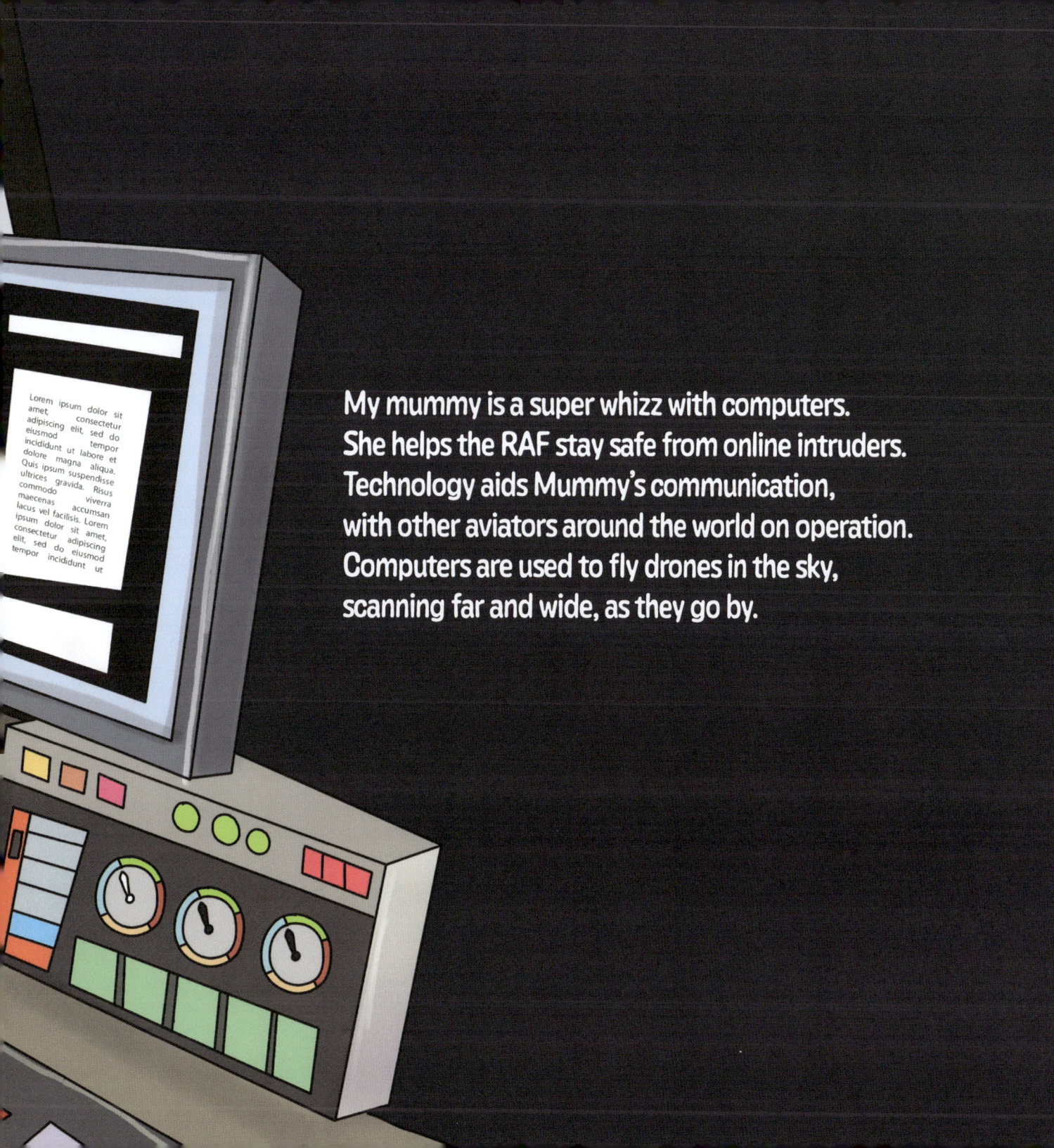

My mummy is a super whizz with computers.
She helps the RAF stay safe from online intruders.
Technology aids Mummy's communication,
with other aviators around the world on operation.
Computers are used to fly drones in the sky,
scanning far and wide, as they go by.

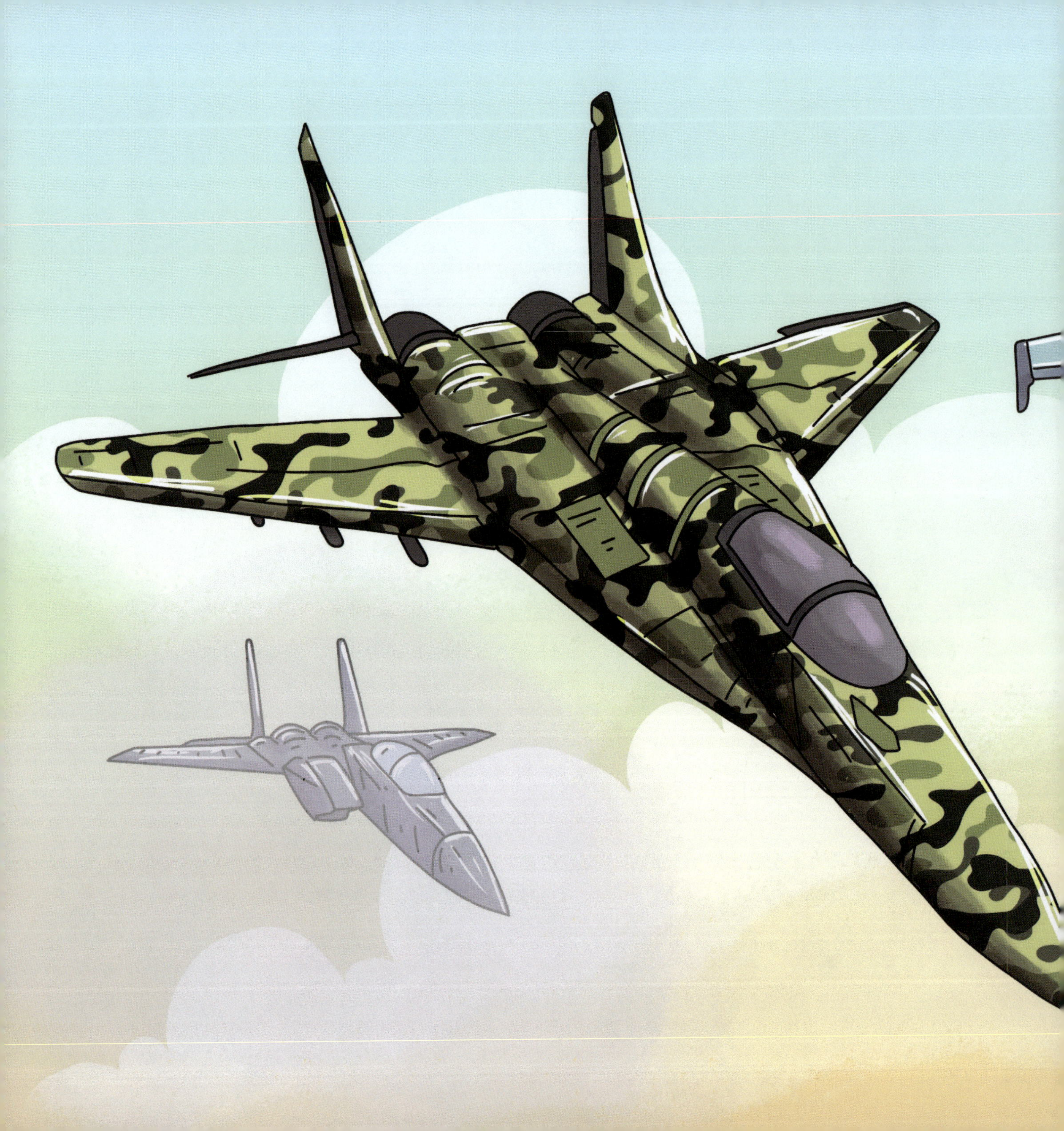

My mummy works for a world of peace,
reinforcing ties between countries to increase
understanding of cultures far and wide,
helping them work together, side by side.
The RAF gives training to distant nations,
fostering peace for future generations.

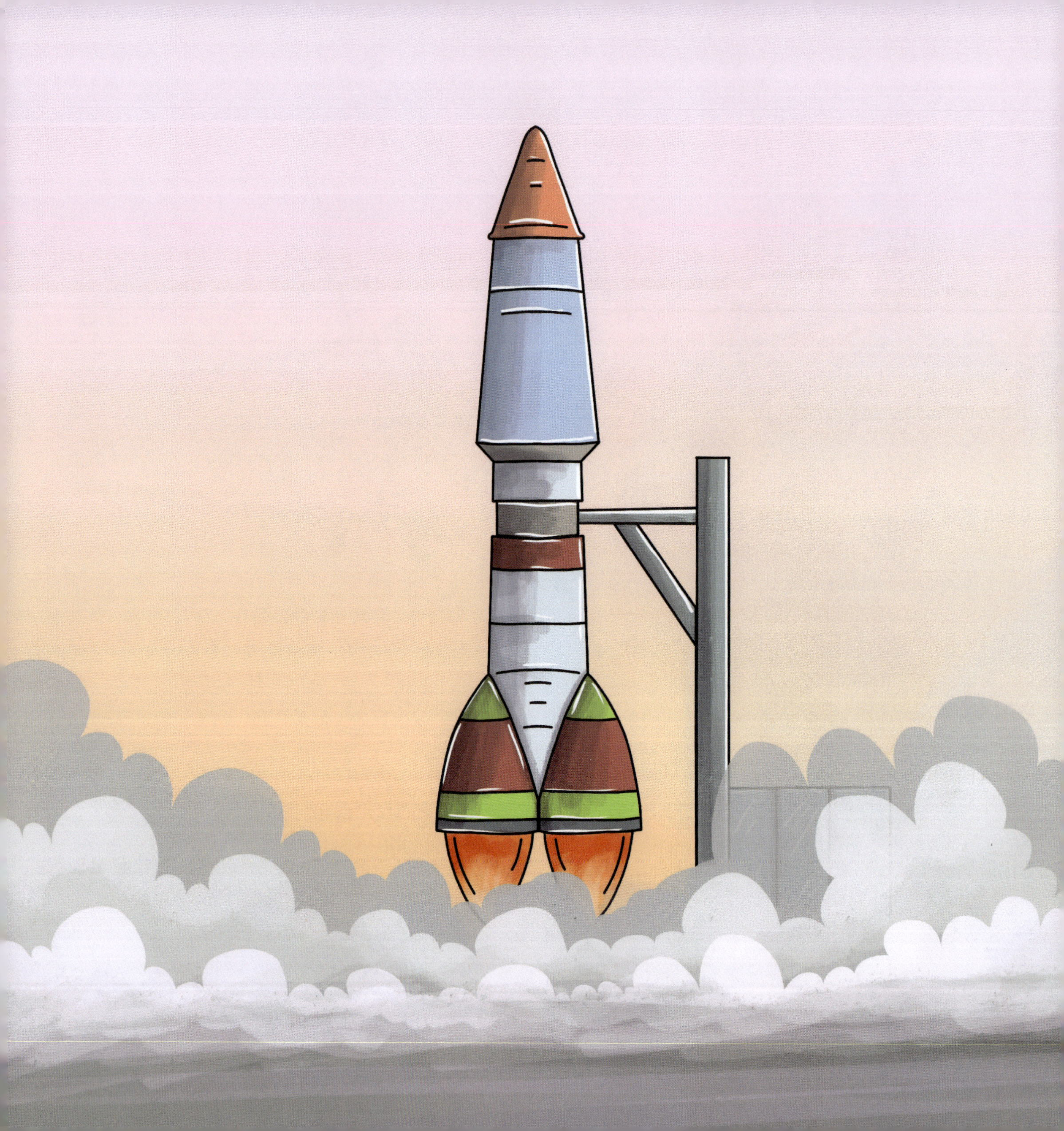

UK Space Command is exciting and new,
supporting the launch of a rocket to space from England to
help with communication from near and far.
RAF satellites floating through space like a star!
An incredible feat of human engineering.
UK Space Command is truly pioneering.

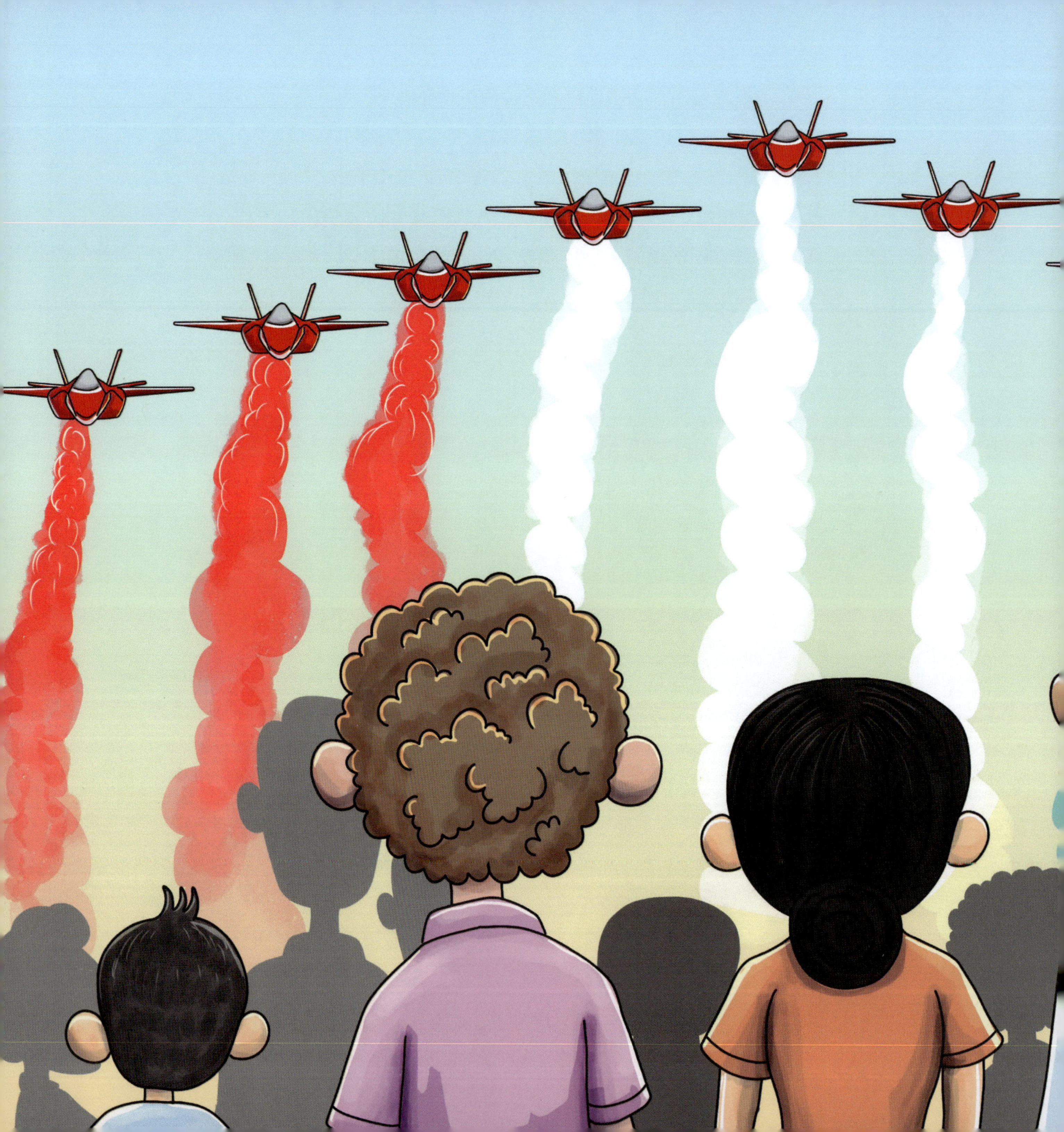

The Red Arrows are the RAF's display team, thrilling crowds with dynamic and supreme manoeuvres, dazzling us with flips and dives, with speed and grace, they soar through the sky. With a trail of smoke of red, blue and white, the jets thunder past like the speed of light.

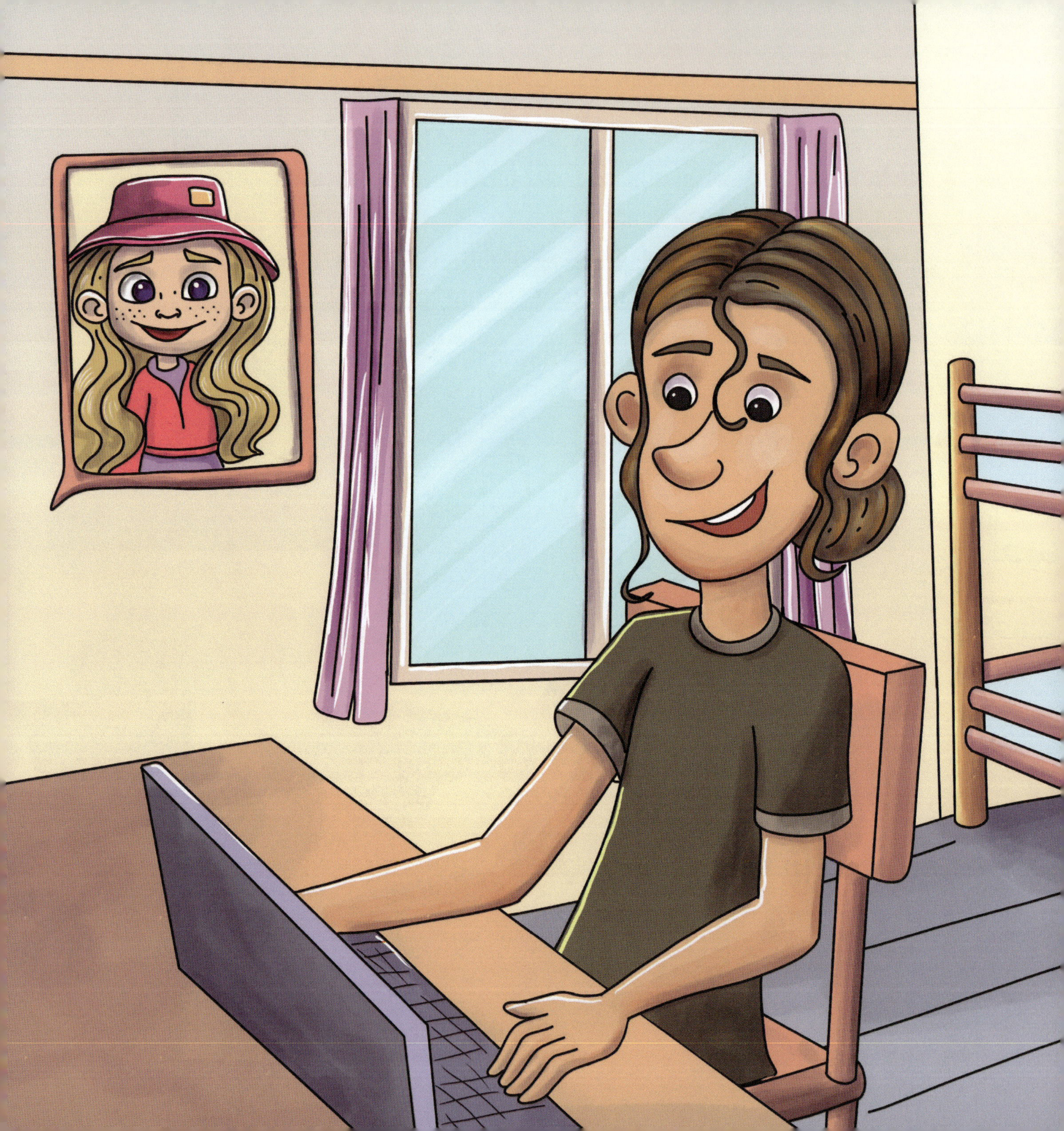

On operations, there's no need to worry about Mummy getting lonely.
She's with her squadron on a base, the accommodation is quite homely.
With photos of me and our whole family on her wall,
she lays in her bed at night and thinks of us all.
There are gyms and restaurants available on the base.
There's even Wi-Fi so we can chat face to face.

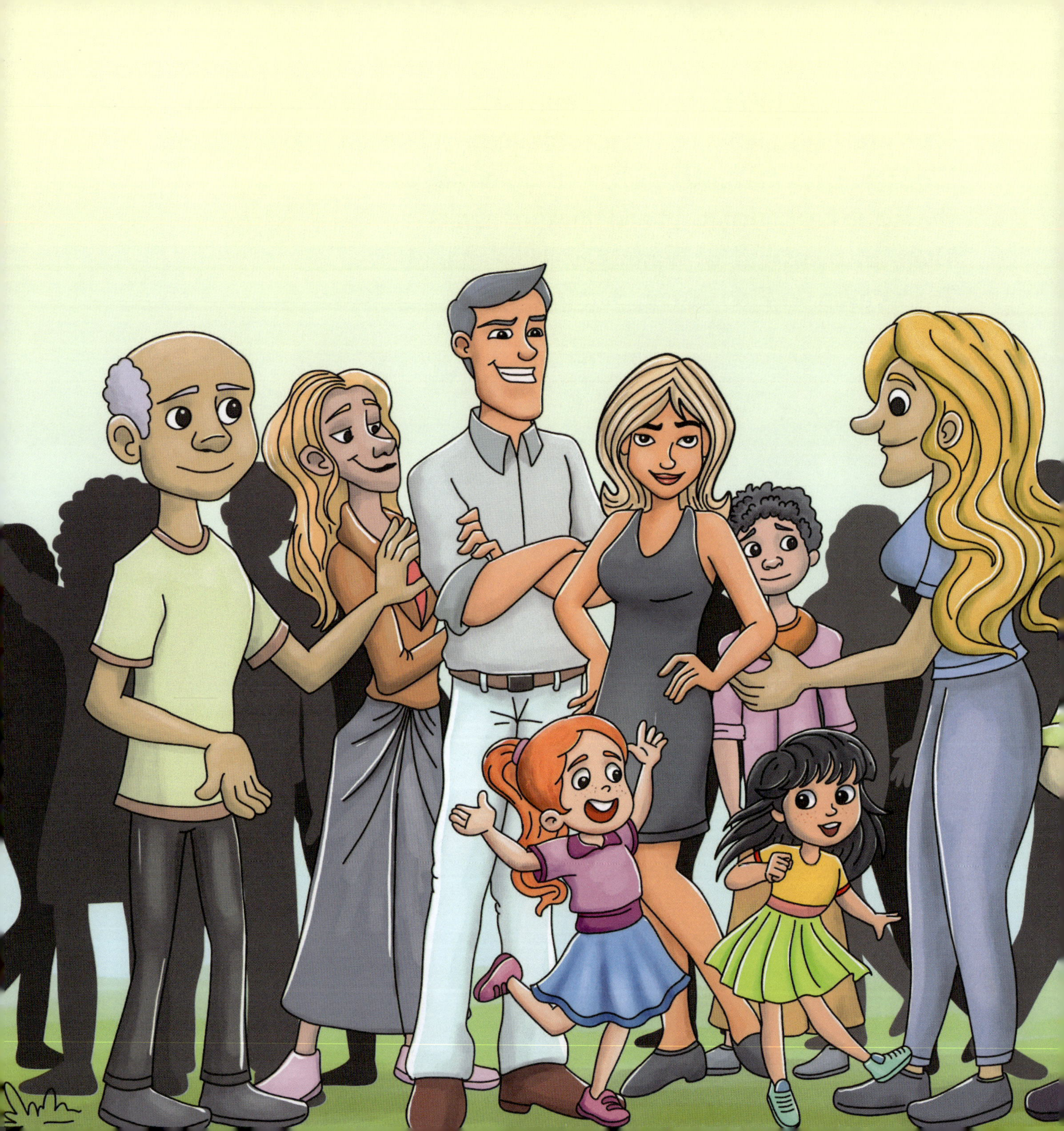

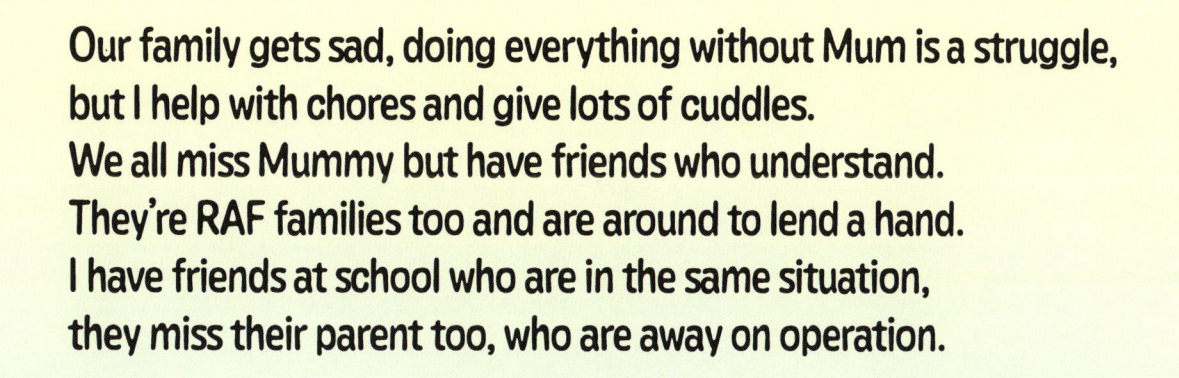

Our family gets sad, doing everything without Mum is a struggle,
but I help with chores and give lots of cuddles.
We all miss Mummy but have friends who understand.
They're RAF families too and are around to lend a hand.
I have friends at school who are in the same situation,
they miss their parent too, who are away on operation.

Military Family Association

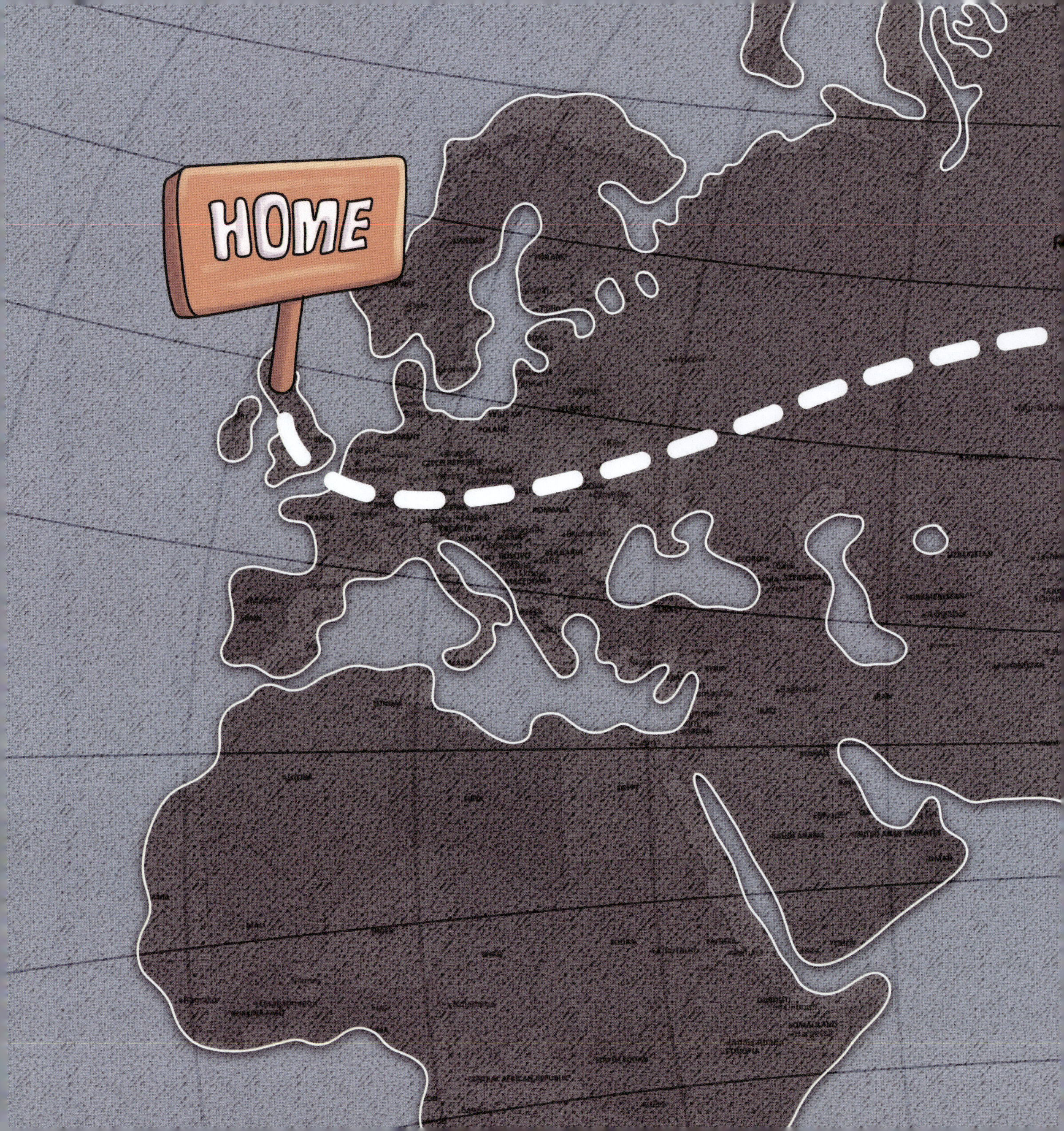
HOME

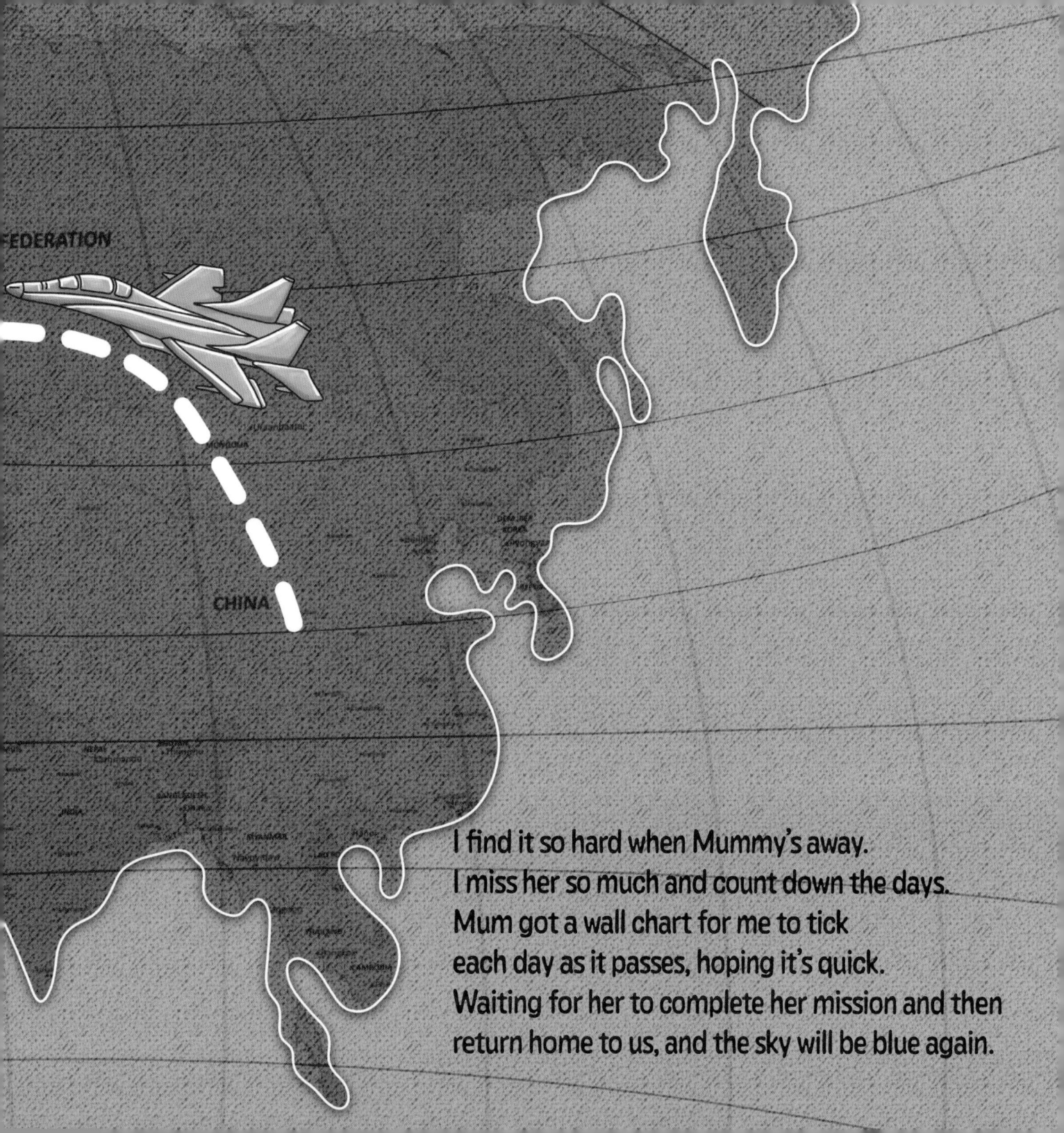

I find it so hard when Mummy's away.
I miss her so much and count down the days.
Mum got a wall chart for me to tick
each day as it passes, hoping it's quick.
Waiting for her to complete her mission and then
return home to us, and the sky will be blue again.

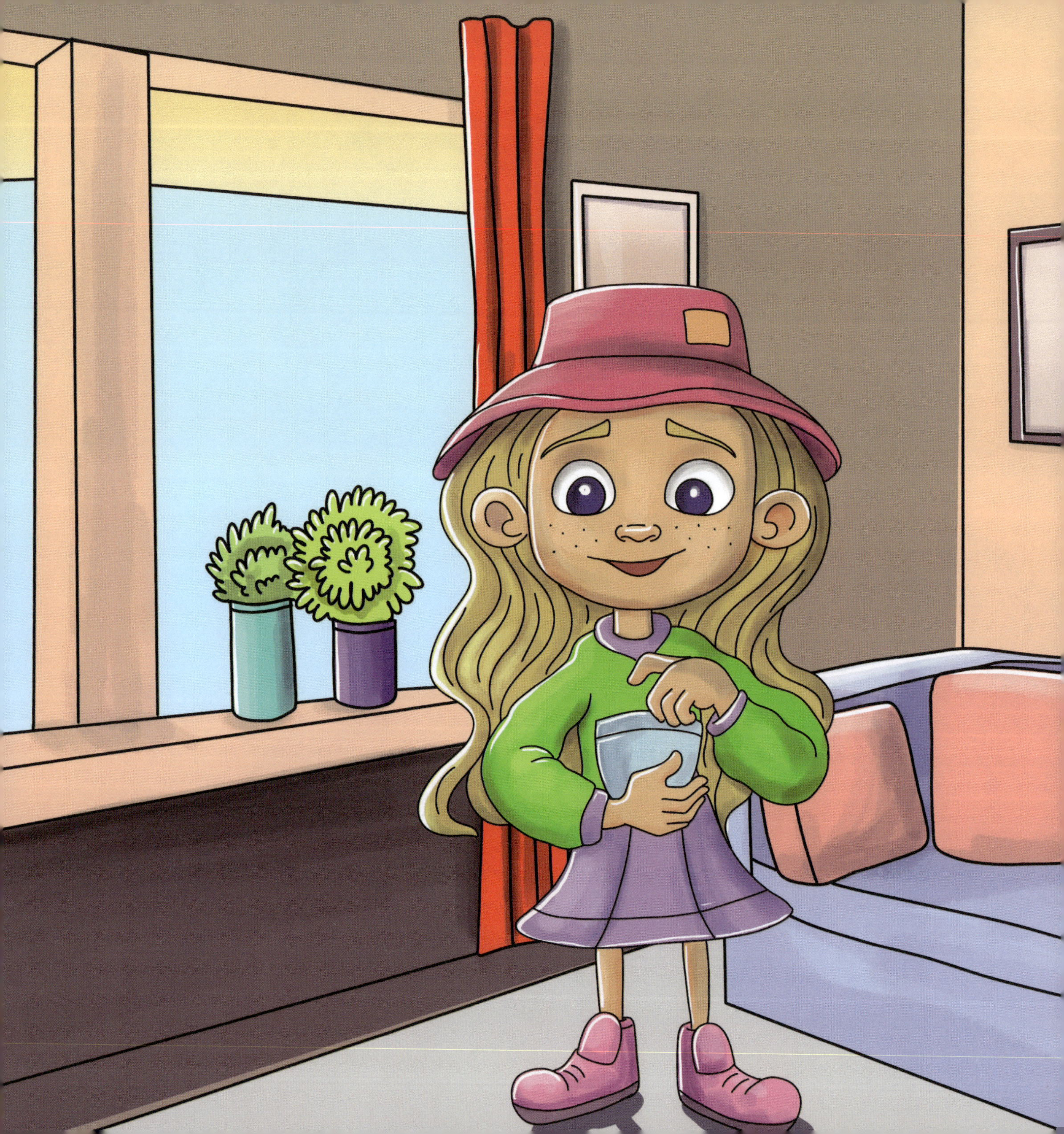

I have a sweet jar and each sweet represents
each day Mummy is away from the day she first went.
Every day I take one sweet savouring its taste.
But for me, it's much sweeter as it's another day faced.
When the day comes that the sweet jar is empty,
I know Mummy's coming home, there'll be celebrations aplenty.

When the sweet jar is empty and the wall chart is done,
I'll be so excited because my mummy's on her way home.
I miss Mummy when she's gone, I can't deny,
but like my mummy, I'm brave in stormy skies.
At bedtime, I look up at the sky and feel safe,
proud to have a mummy who's an aviator in the RAF.

Printed in Great Britain
by Amazon